W9-DGG-384

Sense of Play

by Dana Meachen Rau

illustrated by Doruntina Beqiraj

CAPSTONE EDITIONS
a capstone imprint

To Mom, Dad, and especially Derek, for providing
a childhood that lives in me forever. —D.M.R.

Published by Capstone Editions, an imprint of Capstone
1710 Roe Crest Drive, North Mankato, Minnesota 56003
capstonepub.com

Text copyright © 2023 Dana Meachen Rau
Illustrations copyright © 2023 Doruntina Beqiraj

Library of Congress Cataloging-in-Publication data
is available on the Library of Congress website
ISBN: 9781684466139 (hardcover)
ISBN: 9781684466962 (ebook PDF)

Many thanks to Monica Roe for her feedback on this story.

Designed by Nathan Gassman

Printed and bound in China. PO5377

The house is a hush in early morning.
Everyone's asleep . . .

. . . except Chip.

KNOCK!
KNOCK!

"Wake up, Joy!"
he calls through the wall.

"I'm sleeping,"
Joy mumbles.

Chip smiles.
"Not anymore!"

Breakfast tastes so much better when you make it yourself.

Crunchy cereal out of the box.
Grape juice pours too fast!

"I'm purple," Joy says.

"I'm wet," Chip laughs.

They scrub up with fluffy dry towels
soon sopped and soaked.

Outside, on the hot, humid day,
the pavement smells like sun.
Joy and Chip race.
Legs pumping pedals.
Wind tickling hair.

Rock on the path!

"OUCH!"
Joy cries.

A hug makes it so much better.

chip
and
Joy's
clubhouse

membership
required

Back at home,
time to rest
in the closet cave.

The floor is filled with
fleecy friends and plumpy pillows.

Joy cuddles close.
"It's okay to turn out the light."

She is afraid of the dark,
but not when Chip reads her stories.

Chip reads the little dots in his book.
They are only bumps to Joy.
They are so much more to Chip.
They are words.

Chip and Joy play Guess the Coin.

"A penny! A dime!" Chip says.

"Nope," Chip says.
"Two nickels and a quarter."
Joy wants to be as smart as Chip when she grows up.

Chip and Joy hunt for silly sounds.

PFFFFT!

Fizzy drinks.

KRRRKLE!

Crumpled paper.

CRASH!

Toppled towers.

Sounds are sillier when you make them yourself!

Yeasty perfume reaches their rooms.

Mom and Dad are baking bread!

The dough is a dome in the bowl.
Punching it down is their favorite part.
The spongy, silky, squashy,
sticky dough hugs their fists.

While the bread bakes, they play Guess the Spice.

"Paprika?"
Chip guesses.

"Yes!" Joy says.

She sniffs. "Cinnamon?"

"Try again," he says.

"Nutmeg?"
she guesses.

"You got it!"

The bread is ready and warm and even tastier with butter!
They share, fingers and lips slick with butter too.

At the end of the day, it's not too late for one more game. Boat bed! The ship is decked with blankets, the bedpost a crow's nest.

"To the brig!"
Chip orders.

Joy loves the brig.

"Ahoy,
dust bunnies!"

Mermaids calling! Dolphins leaping!
Chip's bedroom is so much more than a room.

"Your turn to be captain,"
Chip says to Joy.

Creaky worn wood. Salty sea spray. Wide-open waters.

The house is a hush at night.

KNOCK, KNOCK!

"Goodnight,"
Chip calls.

KNOCK, KNOCK!

"Goodnight."
Joy calls back.

Tomorrow will be another day
for so much more than play.

Author's Note

My brother, Derek, and I were constant playmates as kids. He was an early riser and often woke me up through our shared bedroom wall so our day of play could begin as soon as possible.

I have sight, and my brother is Blind. Play for us was an all-senses experience. Outside, we felt the rumble of asphalt as we raced bikes down our quiet street. Our jungle gym screeched at its joints as we swung. In the garden, we knew the tomato plants by their smell.

Inside, we devoured stories. Some we played on his record player, some he read to me in Braille, and some I read to him in print. We also had a large scratch-and-sniff book collection. Tinkertoys were our favorite building toys, and we constructed elaborate cities from them. We also liked the beeps and buzzes of electronic games. His tape recorder was always present, recording sound effects that we'd play back over and over again.

But the best games were when we transformed our bedrooms into anything we could imagine. We didn't need to see the ship or cave or enchanted forest. We could make them real just by wanting them to be.

Like most siblings, we not only played, but we argued and got jealous. We also comforted and helped each other when one of us needed it.

Everyone plays in their own way. I wrote this story to share the fun of my childhood—memorable not just because of how Derek and I played, but also because of how much I loved playing with my dear brother.

Author Bio

Dana Meachen Rau has written more than 350 books for children in a variety of genres, fiction and nonfiction, from picture book to young adult. She also works as an artist and teacher. No matter what she's creating, she tries to approach it with a sense of play. Dana lives in Burlington, Connecticut.

Illustrator Bio

Doruntina is a children's illustrator based in Toronto, Canada. She has a passion for creating warm and charming characters and enjoys experimenting with textures and patterns. Her art is inspired by the magic of everyday moments.